ONE GOOD PUNCH

ONE GOOD PUNCH

RICH WALLACE

LAUREL-LEAF
BOOKS

Published by Laurel-Leaf
an imprint of Random House Children's Books
a division of Random House, Inc.
New York

This is a work of fiction. Names, characters, places, and incidents either are the
product of the author's imagination or are used fictitiously. Any resemblance to actual
persons, living or dead, events, or locales is entirely coincidental.

Originally published in hardcover in the United States by Alfred A. Knopf Books for
Young Readers, New York, in 2007. This edition published by arrangement with
Alfred A. Knopf Books for Young Readers.

Laurel-Leaf and colophon are registered trademarks of Random House, Inc.

Visit us on the Web! www.randomhouse.com/teens

Educators and librarians, for a variety of teaching tools,
visit us at www.randomhouse.com/teachers

The Library of Congress has cataloged the hardcover edition of this work as follows:
Wallace, Rich.
One good punch / Rich Wallace.
p. cm.
Summary: Eighteen-year-old Michael Kerrigan, writer of obituaries for the *Scranton
Observer* and captain of the track team, is ready for the most important season of his
life—until the police find four joints in his school locker, and he is faced with a
choice that could change everything.
ISBN: 978-0-375-81352-8 (trade)—ISBN: 978-0-375-91352-5 (lib. bdg.)
[1. Conduct of life—Fiction. 2. Integrity—Fiction. 3. Track and field—Fiction.
4. Journalism—Fiction. 5. High schools—Fiction. 6. Schools—Fiction. 7. Scranton
(Pa.)—Fiction.] I. Title.
PZ7.W15877One 2007
[Fic]—dc22
2006033270

ISBN: 978-0-440-42260-0 (pbk.)
Reprinted by arrangement with Alfred A. Knopf Books for Young Readers
RL: 6.2
February 2009

Printed in the United States of America
10 9 8 7 6 5 4 3 2
First Laurel-Leaf Edition

For Sandra

SECTION A

NEWS and OPINION

Coal-Mine Fires
Continue to Smolder

PEOPLE KEEP DYING, so my phone never stops ringing. I've made notes in the computer for fourteen obituaries tonight, and I haven't written up a single one. Most I've ever done in a shift is fifteen, and it's only 9:23, so there's plenty more to come.

"*Scranton Observer*. . . . Yeah, we got time. . . . He was a high school valedictorian, and then he worked in the *mines*? . . . Which Legion post? . . . In Jessup? . . . Mercy Hospital; family by his side. Okay. Talk to you later."

I've been doing this job for five months now, and this is the busiest night I've ever had. Officially, I'm an editorial assistant, which used to be called a copy boy and generally means gofer.

I'm a backup phone-answerer for the news department, but mostly I talk to the funeral directors and get information for the next day's obituaries—the dead person's name, age, where they were born, where they lived, surviving relatives, employment history, etc. Also the stuff that makes these things interesting—their hobbies, organizations they belonged to, their World War II–era nicknames (already today I've had Babe, Pops, Hammer, and Dingle). Then I write it up into readable paragraphs for the morning paper, doing it as fast as I can.

"*Scranton Observer*. . . . c-z-y-k? . . . Okay, so 'after a dignified and courageous struggle.' . . . Life member of VFW Post 4921. Where's that again? . . . Lone Pine Hunting Club. . . . Where'd he work? . . . Yeah, call me back with the survivors. No problem."

I'm on a first-name basis with all of the local funeral directors, who call us in the evenings to get their latest clients featured in the paper. I work Friday, Saturday, and Monday nights, which sucks when you're a high school senior— I miss all the parties—but it's undeniably good experience for what I want to do with my life. These were the only shifts available.

"*Scranton Observer*. . . . Yes, Mr. Powell, this is Mike. . . . I haven't written it yet, but I've got my notes right here. . . . Scranton Eagles Memorial Classic at South Side Lanes, 1946. You say he rolled a 282, not 280. . . . Fixed it. Anything else? . . . I've got his brothers Fred in Minooka and Johnny in Dunmore, and a sister Kitty in Green Ridge. And predeceased by a brother Buddy in 1997. . . .

"Yeah, of course we can mention the dogs. . . . Lucy and E-t-h-e-l. They both Labs? . . . Sweet. They gotta be missing him. They let dogs go to funerals, don't they? . . . Oh yeah, I'm running like eight miles a day. I jump on a treadmill at the Y when it's icy, but it's been dry lately. We start working out for real on Wednesday. Can't wait. . . . Thanks. Come see a race if you get a chance."

There are a lot of very old people around this city. Well, obviously there are fewer all the time. But you learn a lot about their lives taking down the information for their final appearance in the newspaper.

You can get a real history lesson reading the obit section every day—all the factories and mills that shut down way before I was born; the huge number of different churches and organizations people belong to (just in the last ten minutes, for example: the Ancient Order of Hibernians, the Polish Women's Alliance, the Red Hat Society, the Olyphant Billiards Association).

Good people—lots of war veterans, lots of faithful parishioners, lots of beloved grandparents. They die at home or in the hospital or a senior center, of old age or cancer or who knows what. The worst cases are when a kid dies in a car accident. Nobody I know yet, but I had to write one a few months ago when two guys from that football team went over the railing on Route 81 in a pickup truck.

You read the obits and you learn about the city's history. But they also get you worrying about its future.

"*Scranton Observer*. . . . Don't call me here, Joey. . . . Because I'm *working*. . . . What kind of emergency? . . . Look in your backpack. I gotta go. . . . Because the phones ring constantly. People die around here every fifteen seconds. . . . *Old* people mostly. . . . I gotta go, man. . . . The other phone is ringing. Get lost."

"*Scranton Observer*. . . . That's me. . . . Sure. One second. . . . Okay—spell that last name. . . . Lifelong resident? . . . So we'll say that he lived briefly in Carbondale before returning to Scranton in 1953. . . . Know when he retired? . . . Okay. Can you hold on a second?"

"*Scranton Observer*. . . . Hi, Mr. Rasmussen. . . . No problem. Can I call you right back? . . . Okay."

"Thanks for holding. I think I knew this guy. Did he umpire Little League games in East Scranton? . . . Right. Right, the gold teeth. Great guy. . . . You can call me back with that. . . . The Friday night deadline is eleven, but we got time. . . . You know where he served? . . . So you're going to want the American flag symbol with this one? . . . You bringing in a photo? . . . No problem. Call me back. We got plenty of time."

It's no wonder the city's population drops with every census. We're still burying former coal miners and textile workers—remnants of long-gone industries. One night last week—both within twenty minutes—I wrote obits for two ladies that were over a hundred years old. Both had lived their *entire lives* in Scranton.

Who replaces them? Probably not me.

I'm out of here in a few months, off to college and then who knows where? If this city had more to offer, I'd probably come back, but as things stand, I can't see it.

Scranton started dying years ago—fading into urban blight. Not collapsing, just losing its gleam. Most of the textile factories closed way back, and although coal-mine fires still smolder under parts of the city, none of the wealth and employment of that industry remain either.

I sometimes picture myself at age thirty, unemployed, sitting on the porch of my parents' house in the evening, drinking a can of beer. It isn't a difficult leap to make— a third of the houses in our neighborhood have someone like that hanging around.

We've had a line of mayors who promised downtown renewal—visions of trendy lofts and premium office space and upscale restaurants and shops. But mostly I run past neighborhood bars like Marty's and the Limerick and all the tire places and used-furniture stores and pawnshops and the unadvertised businesses—there's prostitution and underage clubs and fronts for other stuff. We know where to buy drugs if we wanted to. That's no secret from anybody.

"*Scranton Observer*. . . . This is Mike. . . . Scranton lost. Dunmore won. Prep won. . . . I don't know; this is obits. Hold on, I'll switch you over to sports."

"*Scranton Observer*. . . . God, Joey. It's probably in your locker. . . . That stuff better not be in *my* locker. . . . Midnight if I'm lucky. . . . *Stop* calling me here."

"*Scranton Observer*. . . . Sure thing. From this afternoon? Let me find it. . . . The Elks, the Kiwanis, and the Polka Lights? . . . Oh. L-i-t-e-s. . . . Yeah, I can still get it in. . . . We'll say a long illness. . . . Umm, did he actually die there? . . . I gotta check with an editor; I don't know if we can get away with that. . . . Could just leave it out. . . . I can write around it. Hold on a second."

"*Scranton Observer*. . . . Not from this phone. . . . Hold on."

"Anybody order a pizza?" I yell.

"Hello? Doesn't look like it. . . . We don't have anybody named Charlie. Somebody's jerking you around. . . . No problem."

"Mr. Morrison? . . . Sorry. How about 'after a lengthy battle with an addiction'? Nah. That sounds terrible. We could just put something at the end like 'Donations to alcoholism research appreciated.' They'll figure it out. . . . They found him in the men's room? . . . Yeah, it's a shame. . . . Oh yeah—'a courageous struggle with personal demons.' They'd be writing *my* obit tomorrow. . . . Talk to you later."

Bear with me—I want to be a writer. My dad is a classics professor at the U, and my mom is a poet and freelance magazine writer. My grandmother, who lives three doors away from us, is a historian. We go to all of the productions at the Scranton Cultural Center (no, that's not an oxymoron) and the colleges. I'm familiar with the works of Shakespeare and Hemingway and Bob Dylan. Someday I want to write at least one piece that would stand up to theirs. For now, I'm at the bottom of the ladder as far as creative writing is concerned, but at least I'm in the business, right?

"Yo, Joey. You find it? . . . You suck. . . . If you stashed it there, you're a dead man. . . . They *do* search. . . . They do, too. With dogs. Especially on weekends. . . . It better not be, I swear to God. . . . Keep looking. . . . Find it."

"*Scranton Observer*. . . . Hey, Mr. Salinardi. I can read that part back to you if you want. Hold on. . . . I got it. 'She was a loving grandmother and friend to all, known especially for her pies and hand-knit sweaters. She was a rabid fan of the Philadelphia Eagles.' . . . How about *dedicated* instead of *rabid*? . . . Great. . . . Memorial contributions to the church. No problem. . . . Yeah, I'm looking at Penn State, but I don't think I'd make the team there. So Kutztown maybe, or East Stroudsburg. If they don't have a good track team, forget it. . . . Thanks. See you later."

"*Scranton Observer*. . . . Okay. . . . Francis with an *i* or an *e*? . . . You know what city in Ireland? . . . Came to Scranton in . . . ? . . . You can call me back with it. Where did he work? . . . Got it. . . . Memberships? . . . Friendly Sons of Saint Patrick. Okay. Mr. Delcalzo, can you hold on for just a second?"

"*Scranton Observer*. . . . You suck, Joey. Why did you put it *there*? . . . They find that stuff, I'm dead."

"*Scranton Observer*. . . . Oh, right. . . . Yeah, you already gave me the Sons of Saint Patrick. . . . Bridge, gardening, and ceramics. . . . Okay. . . . I'll wait. No problem."

Dammit, Joey. You're an idiot.

The sports guys are still finishing up when I've turned in the night's final obituary to my editor, so I walk over to that end of the newsroom. The sports department always holds things up by five or ten minutes, but I guess by now they've built that into the press schedule.

There are lots of strange characters in a newsroom, but the sports department tops them all. Fat, nasty Larry is sitting there in his undershirt, scratching the pimples on his back with a ruler. He's the assistant sports editor, and he's waiting for Andy to finish his write-up of the Scranton-Hazleton play-off game.

"Hurry up with that thing so we can nominate it for a Pulitzer," Larry says.

Andy smirks and nods. "Last sentence," he says. Andy is a shirt-and-tie guy, polite and professional. He's only two years out of Penn State, and you know it won't be long before he's at one of the Philadelphia papers or a magazine. No way he'll be sitting here in thirty years, bored out of his mind, leaking pus, editing high school sports news like Larry.

I don't think Larry is the type of guy who ever really got it, who ever understood how important sports are. I am totally driven by winning the 800 meters at the district meet and getting to the states. Then winning a medal. A big part of me is driven by winning the state gold. That's so far-fetched that I wouldn't say it to anyone. But I think it can happen.

On the wall behind Larry is a poster of Gerry McNamara, the kid from Scranton who as a freshman led Syracuse University to the NCAA basketball title a few years ago. He almost single-handedly lifted this city up for a while. Busloads of fans would travel the two hours from Scranton to Syracuse for his games over the next three years. For his final home game, sixty buses—*sixty*—made the trek.

There's an editorial from the *Observer* taped next to the poster, from the day after McNamara's final collegiate game. It says that the guy "embodied the grit and determination of this entire region, particularly the city he calls home."

From this end of the newsroom, you can look out over our gritty, ever-struggling city, which is dead this close to midnight. There are pockets of activity around the bars, but most of the streets are virtually empty and windswept.

Larry notices that I'm looking out the window. "The Electric City," he says scornfully. "The greatest city in this corner of Lackawanna County."

I shrug. "It has its charms."

"Oh yeah." He stands up and waddles over to the window. He stares down at Flaherty's Pub, right across the street from the Observer building. "There's one of them charms behind the bar. . . . I'll be home soon, Mildred," he croons, pointing toward the bartender. "Make sure that keg is cold."

Since I'm an athlete, you'd think I'd want to be working in the sports department, but I'll pass. There are a couple of young guys like Andy with ambition who'll use this as a jumping-off point for something better, but mostly it's older burnouts like Larry who've been here forever and spend their time drinking and arguing over baseball trivia.

How can anybody do the same damn job for thirty years?

Rico and Jay are standing on the corner across from the square as I walk home from work, so I go over. They're probably drunk—they do too much of that—but maybe it's the final fling before practice starts. I never hang out with them (except a couple of times when I *did* get drunk), but track gives us some common ground, especially since we're all on the same relay team.

For me, the lure of track has always been to assert myself as an individual, but sometimes you can take four guys who wouldn't quite make it to the states on their own, lump them together in a relay, and have big-time results. That's what we're thinking will happen this spring.

"Kerrigan," Jay says. He's taller than me, with straight blond hair and a perpetual smirk. He's faster than I am, too, but not by much. And I always beat him in any race longer than a sprint.

"What's going on, boys?" I ask.

Rico is leaning against the building, hands in his pockets. He's new here; arrived in our freshman year. Like most of the small influx of newcomers to the city, he's brownish. "We're kind of wasted," he says with a smile.

I shake my head. "The season's here." Neither one of these guys is as committed as I am, and that always pisses me off. I don't really know if I'm fast enough or strong enough to win the districts on my own; if I'm going to the states, it'll probably be on the relay. And I don't want anything to interfere with that. These guys need to step up as much as I do.

"Don't worry, champ," Rico says. "A few beers ain't gonna set us back."

Jay starts laughing. He holds up his hand for Rico to smack. Then he turns to me. "We ran our asses off this afternoon. Like we been saying all along, we're going to the *states*. We're gonna medal, too."

"And *then* we'll get drunk for real," Rico adds. "We'll even get *your* puritan ass wasted again."

I roll my eyes. I've got this reputation as a straight boy—almost never drunk, never in trouble. It's why Coach named me captain, even though there are people on the team with better athletic credentials.

"Then we'll get you and your girlfriend drunk and watch the sparks fly," Rico says, laughing. "See if you two can finally figure out how the parts are supposed to fit together."

He's referring to my best friend, Shelly. *Not* my

girlfriend. We hang out together all the time; have for years. People wonder why we haven't taken it very far. They don't know everything, but it's true we haven't done much. You don't go from playing Monopoly with her and her parents to having sex.

"Shelly knows how the parts work," Jay says. "She just likes girls' parts better."

There's that wrinkle, too. I don't know if it's true, but it's been the rumor forever.

"Who cares?" Rico says. He puts his hand on my shoulder and squeezes. "Get her drunk enough, she'll do anybody. She's a girl; go for it."

"Just be prepared to get your ass kicked if she don't like it, Mike," Jay says. "She's one tough bitch."

No, she isn't. "You're a jerk," I say. "I need to get home. See you in school."

I start walking away. They're both giggling. "Read a nice bedtime story," Jay calls after me. "Nothing too scary or suggestive."

City Moves Forward, Slips Back

My FAVORITE RUN is to get out of East Scranton and head into Green Ridge toward Dunmore, really working those hills out there. Saturday morning I hit Boulevard Avenue and head over to Woodlawn Street, which climbs steeper than any of them and has a grass median up the center, lined with sycamores. You pound that hill for three hard blocks, crossing Capouse and Wyoming, then zigzag onto the pavement past the bigger houses on Jefferson all the way up to Madison. The legs are burning and your chest is heaving and you have to pump your arms like you're doing curls with forty-pound dumbbells. And if you wimp out in a race after completing workouts like that every week, then I'm sorry, you just ain't cut out for running.

It hurts like hell. I love it.

That's almost a mile uphill, and it gets progressively harder. The tightly packed Victorian houses on either side are neat and lived-in, with steep cement steps and wrought-iron railings. A lot of them are decorated with cardboard shamrocks and green balloons. Saint Patrick's Day is a few weeks away, and this *is* still Scranton, after all.

But things are changing.

Look at our 4-by-800-meter relay team, the one we expect to score big this spring. Leadoff guy is from Trinidad; Rico moved here two years ago from the Bronx; Jay is from some city in New Jersey. The anchor guy—me—is the lone true Scrantonian, the one "lifelong resident of the East Side of Scranton," as we say in the obits.

But you want a few bright spots? Look around. Things *did* get better, at least for a few years. I'm no sociologist, but I can trace it back to the season things started changing for us. I was still in middle school, but I felt it. It was like the entire city snapped back and realized that we didn't have to keep fading. We could take seven steps forward for every six steps back instead of the other way around.

I'm a sports fan, and above all I'm an athlete, so maybe I'm not objective about this. But my grandmother caught it, and all of our neighbors, and the cops and the storekeepers and everybody walking the streets a few years ago when that Irish-Catholic kid from Scranton, USA, led Syracuse to the title.

My goal is to follow the path that Gerry McNamara took. My sports are cross-country and track—lower-profile but just as tough.

Sometimes I'm running not quite as hard as I ought to be, letting my mind drift and not putting forth the effort I meant to, and I'll happen past little Bishop Hannan High School or some other place that reminds me of McNamara—that toughness, the focus that made you certain he'd nail consecutive three-pointers or get that crucial steal—and suddenly I'm running a whole lot faster, and I can't wait to reach one of those killer hills and just kick its ass all the way to the top.

It's at moments like that when I know I can take this running thing far. State meet this spring; All-American in college.

Scranton is the butt of jokes in movies and TV shows, as if it's all polka and kielbasa and bowling alleys and pool rooms and former miners with black lung and no teeth. Give me a break. That's only 90 percent of it. Maybe not even.

Laugh if you want, or sneer. But check the results of the state track championships this May and see if my name isn't there.

My grades aren't that good, by the way, and so far my athletic performances aren't either. I did almost get to the state meet in cross-country. I finished eighth in the district and have the medal hanging on the wall of my bedroom. But I won't be running for Villanova or Georgetown or

Providence next year. No problem; I'll keep developing anyway.

I'm in the best shape of my life, ready to set records. A power runner—not big, but with a low center of gravity and good core strength. A guy who can keep going when things get difficult.

I'm as tough as this city. I *am* this city in every cell of my body. It's spelled r-e-s-i-l-i-e-n-c-e.

Like the fires in the coal mines, we're virtually impossible to extinguish.

After my run, I try to slip into the school through the locker room, but no dice. Usually the place would be busy on a Saturday morning with sports teams practicing, but the basketball teams are all done and only a couple of wrestlers advanced to the regionals. So the gym is locked up.

The side doors are locked, too. I flag down one of the custodians—Eddie, a good guy, been here forever, always asks me about track—but he says he's been told not to let anybody into the school.

"Something must be up," he says at the door, wiping his nose with his wrist. "They said not to let anybody in for any reason."

"No problem," I say. "I left a pair of running shoes in my locker, but I've got others."

Would have been nice to clean Joey's little surprise out of my locker and rest easy for the weekend, but I won't sweat it.

So I walk the three blocks home, up the hill and on the outskirts of the downtown business area. My clothes are damp from the run and I'm thirsty and hungry, and I try not to think about what might be going on in the school. They've been doing drug sweeps every month or two.

Nobody would suspect me anyway. I'm an athlete; I've never been in trouble; I don't associate with trouble-makers.

Ask anybody around that school: I'm almost too good to be true.

I get cleaned up and eat some leftover chicken wings and head to Shelly's house. Her mother is a nurse at the high school, and I figure she might have a way of getting me to my locker.

I've known Shelly since fourth grade, when she sat behind me in Mrs. Palumbo's class at Jefferson School. She had a bad cold one day, so her nose was clogged and it affected her speech. Also her sense of smell, which turned out to be a good thing.

The congestion did not affect her hearing, so when Jimmy Risalvato in the aisle next to us farted loudly, she poked me in the shoulder and asked, "Can you spell that?"

She meant *smell*, but like I said, her speech was impaired. And I took it literally.

I turned around and said, "P-f-u-r-r-d-t?"

She laughed so hard Mrs. Palumbo made her go out in the hall for ten minutes.

Ever since then, I've been spelling fart sounds to her.

F-a-a-a-r-d-t.

P-i-f-f-e-r-r-d-s-s-t.

B-r-e-d-i-f-f-r-i-d-i-f-e-r-r-r-t.

It never gets old.

Anyway, Shelly's mother isn't home, and Shelly says there's probably no way her mom could get access to the high school on a weekend without a very good reason.

I ask Shelly if she's up for going to a movie on Sunday night at the Cultural Center. They show art films and foreign stuff the fourth Sunday of every month.

"Sure, Mike. It's a date." She puts her hand on my shoulder.

I nod. It's not a date. We'll just be hanging out, like usual.

Shelly is cool, and she's cute and athletic, with dark hair and a sweet smile. But we've been friends for so long that it's kind of like hanging out with a cousin. Too close for anything much sexual to happen. I get tempted and we've experimented, but it doesn't feel quite right.

She keeps her hand there for a few seconds, looking at my eyes. I look down and feel my face getting hot. She laughs when she sees me blushing. And she steps closer, right up against me. "We left some unfinished business last time," she whispers.

"Yeah, I guess we did," I say. But maybe we'll just leave it that way.

"We'll say unexpectedly. . . . After being stricken at home. . . . Teamsters. Which local? . . . Okay. . . . Attended Minooka schools. . . . He belong to a church? . . . There's a Saint *Rocco*? . . . Got it. . . . Friends may call. . . . Okay."

"*Scranton Observer.* . . . You know her age? . . . A hundred and two? Wow. . . . Hobbies or anything? . . . Get out! Parachuting? Until her late seventies. . . . Hey, Mr. Powell, can you hold on a second?"

"Be right with you, Tucker."

"I'm back. . . . Okay. . . . Her husband died *seventy-four* years ago? . . . Where'd she work? . . . We can say 'including the Duchess Underwear Company, Scranton Lace, and the Jaunty Fabric Corporation.' I love that one. . . . Yeah, call me back. . . . The Saturday night deadline is early, so only till about ten."

Tucker is our police-beat guy on the weekends. He's a senior journalism major at the U, but he's writing a crime novel, so the cop beat is great research for him. He tries to talk like a hardened reporter, almost to the point of being a cliché. He even wears an old fedora and a skinny black tie. It's all part of the fun for him.

I walk over and ask, "What's up?"

Tucker sits back in his chair and puts one foot up against his gray metal desk. "Drug sweep at East Scranton High, Mr.

Kerrigan. The hallowed halls of learning where you go to school."

"Really?" My stomach gets tight.

"Yeah. Pretty routine; they found pot in a few lockers."

"They arrest anybody?"

"Not yet. And this is *strictly* confidential, bro. They don't even want us to report anything until at least Monday, after they confront the perps."

"How many kids?"

"I don't know. I gotta rap with a dick at headquarters later to get the facts. But it didn't sound like any huge thing. Mostly just users, not dealers. Five or six people involved, maybe."

"Probably just some scumbags," I say, but I feel a little shaky.

The cop-beat desk is basically a bank of phones and computer terminals in the middle of the newsroom, so there's no wall to lean against. I take a seat on an empty desk across from Tucker. "What do they do to the people they catch?" I ask.

"Depends how much dope they had, I guess." Tucker takes out a cigarette and puts it in his mouth. You can't smoke in the building, but he's always gnawing on an unlit one. "They get bigger fines for it being at a school, but probably the kids are still minors anyway."

"What does the school do, I mean?"

Tucker shrugs. The cigarette hangs from his lip. "Suspend the perps, as far as I know. Or expel them, especially if they think anybody was dealing."

I just nod. "Let me know if you hear anything else. . . . And, uh, just curious, if you talk to anybody from the school, find out what they do to the kids."

"Will do."

"Hello? Huh? Oh yeah, this is the *Scranton Observer*. Sorry. . . . Sure, no problem. . . . Where did he die? . . . After being stricken at home. . . . Okay. . . . I'm sorry, what was that again? . . . An army veteran of World War II, serving in the Airborne Division. . . . Any survivors? . . . You said *Brian*? . . . Oh. *Byron*. Sorry. . . . Lithua-n-i-a-n R.C. Church. . . . Right. . . . Right. . . . Sorry, what was that last thing you gave me? . . . Valley View Coal Company. . . . Right. . . . No, I'm okay. Just distracted by something. . . . Lettered in football and baseball at Scranton Central High School. . . . Yeah, that sounds like quite a life. . . . Donations to the American Diabetes Association. . . . Got ya. . . ."

"Scranton Pride" Campaign Produces Mixed Results

THERE AREN'T A TON of homeless people in Scranton, but they're out there. I see the same few every time I walk home from the *Observer* after midnight. Charlie is usually in the doorway of the old National Bank building; Santa is on a bench by the courthouse; Wiley is wandering around the square.

Like I said, there aren't many other signs of life this time of night, especially in the winter, so these guys are almost a welcome sight. Walk along Mulberry or any other downtown street away from the courthouse square and you're astounded by all the vacant spaces. Eight or ten buildings in a row—beautiful brick and stone buildings—and the storefronts are empty except for maybe a little shoe-repair shop or a sandwich place in the middle of the block. The windows are covered in brown paper and big FOR RENT signs. The slogan OFFICE/RETAIL SPACE AVAILABLE is as ubiquitous as those green-and-gold Scranton Pride banners.

I did a term paper about the city in tenth grade. The one thing that sticks in my mind from that research is that, in the early 1900s, *National Geographic* said Scranton was the richest city of its size *in the entire frickin' world*. All that iron and steel and coal. There's been a heck of a big drop-off since then, let me tell you.

But there's always a big renovation job going on somewhere, some plumber's or bricklayer's pickup truck on the sidewalk and a big yellow chute from an upstairs window leading down to a Dumpster.

And then you get closer to the square and there are *so many* banks and a bunch of restaurants and a handful of jewelry shops near the Lackawanna County Courthouse. So there must be a lot of money around here somewhere.

I gotta call Joey when I get home. I forgot to bring my cell, but I'm going to ream him out good for the dope in my locker. I'm figuring my clean record and the fact that I'm a sports guy is going to help make this go away quietly.

If it doesn't, then my life is going to change in a hurry.

Our house is small and gray, halfway up the hill a few blocks from the university and basically indistinct. The front light is on and my parents are asleep, so I grab my cell phone and go out to the street. Joey picks up on the first ring.

"They did a drug sweep," I say.

"Who did?"

"The cops."

"Today?"

"Yeah."

"Damn," Joey says. "They find anything?"

"Yeah."

"You get arrested?"

"No. Not yet anyway."

"Then how do you know about it?" he asks.

"A reporter told me. Where are you?"

"I'm on Gibson Street. Walking home."

"Head down this way. Go over to Jefferson and come toward my house. I'll meet you."

I hang up on him before he can respond, but he better show up. I never said he could put anything like that in my locker. It wasn't my stuff. And no way would I ever put it in my locker even if it was.

We meet up in front of one of the university buildings. Most of the campus is off by itself, but there are several buildings on the edge of the downtown like this one.

Joey's got this big shit-eating grin as if this is real funny, but he's got nothing at stake like I do. He's not going to college; he hasn't got any senior-year track season to worry about. He'll be lucky if he graduates.

"Dude," he says, putting out his fist to meet mine but looking over to the side. He's shorter than I am and tries to dress like a hood, but he was one of the most uncool kids around until last year, and now he overdoes it.

"So, fill me in," he says. "What'd the man say?"

"Not much. Just that they found drugs in some lockers and haven't arrested anybody yet."

"So that doesn't mean they found anything in yours. They probably went right to lockers like Freddy's."

"Freddy's not that stupid," I say. "Hardly *anybody* is." And by that I mean that Joey is one of the few.

"Like I said, they'd never suspect you," he says. "Nobody would think you'd have drugs in your locker."

"That's because I *wouldn't*. What were you thinking, man?"

"That it was probably the safest place in the school to stash it."

Joey has my locker combination because I let him put books there sometimes between classes so he doesn't have to lug them around. My locker is right in the center of the main hall. His is down in the depths.

We were friends way back in fifth grade before *any* of us were cool—always playing video games together at my house and talking about sports during school. I never quite shook him. Last summer he moved up a notch in status when he started hanging out with a party crowd. I would run into him on the street at night and he'd smell like pot or beer. But most of the time he was still the same geeky little guy, so we stayed friends, more or less.

I've been to his house. Not the type of place you want to hang out at. His parents are both alcoholics, and they fight a lot. Joey gets yelled at with good reason and not, and there's always a pile of dishes in the sink and a cracked window or a leak. It's no surprise he's never home anymore except to sleep.

So I could turn him in if I get questioned. Yeah, it was in my locker, but they'd believe me if I said who put it there. And I'd be telling the truth. I never had possession, no money had changed hands. Technically, all the guilt is on him.

"Look," he says. "Just deny everything. Say you have no idea how it got there. You could get twenty-five teachers to vouch for your character. 'It's clearly a frame-up,' they'll say. 'Thomas and Catherine's little boy would never do a thing like that.'"

I shake my head slowly and watch a couple of cars go by. I want to smack him, but he's too innocently sleazy.

"You gonna incriminate me?" he asks, making it sound funny even though I think he's worried that I will.

"You suck," I tell him for the fiftieth time since this happened. Where do you draw the line with your integrity? Do you protect yourself or your friend?

He rolls his eyes. "It'll probably just blow over anyway," he says. "We don't know nothing about it, all right? Anybody could slip a few joints between the slots of a locker."

"So just lie about it, huh?"

"Believe me, Mike, they'd *want* you to lie. No way do they want to find drugs in a locker like yours. They do those sweeps to get rid of people like Freddy. Or me. No way they wanna screw with captains of the sports teams or anything like that. That hits the papers and it looks bad for everybody. But if they catch the 'delinquents' in my crowd, then the school looks good for weeding out the scum, right?"

"Maybe."

"You got nothing to worry about. I guarantee they didn't even check your locker," he says. "Believe me."

"Yeah. Maybe."

He looks me in the eye finally, then checks his watch. "Whatever happens," he says, "just do me a favor and leave me out of it."

SECTION B

LIFESTYLES
and OBITUARIES

Anxiety Has Negative Effect
on Performance, Report Finds

I DIDN'T SLEEP TOO WELL but managed a few hours and then woke up suddenly raring to go. The sun is shining, and it doesn't look too cold out at all.

My parents have already gone off to church—I make my appearances there on Christmas and Easter—and I'm not in any mood for conversation anyway. So I eat some toast and an orange and lace up the running shoes and head out, figuring some easy miles will calm me down and give me some perspective.

The first few miles are very low-intensity, no effort at all because I'm still thinking hard about the situation and what it might cost me. But I'm starting to heat up now, feeling better.

I'm following part of the course for the Steamtown Marathon, which they hold every October. The course starts out in the woods, then makes its way through Carbondale and the valley and eventually finishes here in downtown Scranton. The running magazines and Web sites consider it one of the best smaller marathons in the nation. I'd like to run it someday, but probably not until after college.

I can see the high school in the distance, and I know there's no better therapy than to get on the track, to hammer out a few 200-meter segments and prepare myself for the spring. I'm all warmed up and ready to roll, so I head down the hill and through the parking lot and through the gates of the stadium.

There's a strong wind—there's always a wind here, since the bleachers on either side funnel it right along the homestretch—but fighting that can only make me tougher.

I stop and stretch for a few seconds, take a deep breath, then hear the crack of the starter's pistol in my head and race into the first turn, picturing the crowd of runners and hearing the yells of my teammates and my coach and the spectators. You have to get out fast in an 800, establish yourself as the guy to beat, the one who has the balls to say, "You want it? Just try to take it from me."

The 800 is two hard laps—maybe the hardest event in track and field. It's close to an all-out sprint, but nobody on Earth can really sprint the whole thing. It's a test of your resolve, actually, how close you can come to holding that speed for that long.

So as you move onto the backstretch of the first lap, you've taken the lead and fought your way to the inside lane, and your elbows are riding high because you're not afraid to use them to keep your position, and your eyes are set straight ahead, but you're aware of who's around you, who thinks they can hang with your pace.

And you're running hard toward the 200-meter mark, knowing how you'll surge on the next turn to string out the runners behind you. The pace is steady and fast. You're just outside your comfort zone, but you've prepared for this so many times that it's become second nature.

I reach the end of the straightaway and slow to a jog. I'm not doing a full 800-meter race today; the point of practicing it in segments is as much psychological as physical. So I'll run an easy half lap between each segment, envisioning the second fast 200-meter interval as the completion of the first lap of the race. The third one is the first half of the second lap; the fourth one takes you to the finish.

There are a couple of joggers in the outside lanes, but they're not in my way, so I couldn't care less. The American flag outside the school is flapping like crazy in the wind.

Start the second one and get right into your zone—almost relaxed but moving at a good clip. The runners with you are contemplating their strategy—let this guy set the pace or try to take over? Put it to him now or wait for a finishing kick?

Relax your shoulders; lean slightly into that turn. Then move out from the rail on the straightaway, to the middle of the lane, forcing anyone who has the nerve to try to pass you to move out even farther. But hold that lead; don't let them by. Make 'em try to move past you on the turn if they dare.

Run smooth on the straightaway. Pick up the pace as you're heading into the second lap. Let everybody know you're just getting started.

My heart is beating hard and my breathing is quick as I slow down again, but my body feels good. The blood is really pumping in my arms, and my legs feel light and springy. It'll be a great season ahead. The best of my life.

I'm focused now, and this pattern of racing is being recorded and embedded in my soul. The third one is crucial—anybody can hang on for a lap, then muster something at the end for a kick. But the 800 is won or lost on the third 200 by the one who's strong enough and tough enough to keep the pace going and then has enough left over to sprint.

So I hold my form—make sure my shoulders aren't hunching up and my stride isn't getting too short. Keep working; don't fight it, just relax if you can and keep running.

And the fourth one. It's only 200 meters now; I've run that distance a million times. They're chasing me, cursing in their heads and reaching as deep as they can, but I'm pulling away, I'm crushing them. It hurts like hell, but I refuse to fold. Harder and faster, right through the finish line.

I am exhausted. I am in pain. But I can't wait to start racing for real. I can't wait. I can't wait. I can't wait.

Thomas M. Kerrigan

Thomas M. Kerrigan, 51, a lifelong resident of this city, has not died yet. He is an associate professor in the Classics Department at the University of Scranton.

He attended Scranton schools and graduated from Addison College in Boston. He later earned a master's degree at Marywood University and a Ph.D. from Temple.

Friends and relatives would describe Dr. Kerrigan as a rather stiff and humorless individual. He has no hobbies to speak of, but he delights in subtly demeaning the speaking faults of those around him. He finds slang and abbreviations particularly distasteful but will stoically endure them with only the most minor complaints.

His son, Michael, recalled a recent exchange between Dr. Kerrigan and his beloved wife, Catherine.

"Honey," said Mrs. Kerrigan, "would you please take the burgers out of the fridge?"

Dr. Kerrigan cleared his throat and replied in an even tone, "Yes, I will gladly take the *ham*burgers out of the *refrigerator*."

Also surviving is Dr. Kerrigan's mother, Ann Kerrigan, of Scranton. He was predeceased by his father, Daniel Kerrigan, in 1991.

Dr. Kerrigan is a parishioner of Saint Anthony's R.C. Church, Scranton, and makes the effort to attend at least once a month.

Expert Links Cheating
to Maturity Level

"HEY, SPORT," my dad says as I enter the house. He's got the *Observer* and the *New York Times* spread out on the kitchen table, and he's listening to National Public Radio.

"Just reading some of your work," he says, bending the paper toward me to show me the obituary page.

"Some fine pieces of journalism, huh?"

"Excellent," he says. He sets the paper down. "It *is* good work. Really. I expect that the admissions departments will take note of that."

"Hope so."

I'm waiting to hear from Penn State and a few of the smaller Pennsylvania colleges, and my dad keeps reminding me how much he loved the little private school in Massachusetts where he got his undergraduate degree. Great school for creative writing, he says. But I checked Addison online, and the track program is terrible. So I applied there to make him happy, but no way I'm going.

I could also go to the U, as he frequently reminds me. But they don't even have a track team, and I don't want to spend four more years at home.

My dad has tufty gray hair and a habit of squeezing his eyes shut quickly before he speaks. He says he had absolutely no interest in athletics until I started competing in track, and even now I don't think he gets it. So he can't understand why it's the most important item on my where-to-go-to-college checklist. His priorities for college and graduate school were strictly about academics. Makes sense, I know. But it's my life, and I plan to enjoy it.

I should mention that despite his lack of interest in sports and his alleged noncompetitive nature, he tends to cheat when we go bowling. We only bowl about twice a year. He doesn't directly fix his score—you can't really do that with the automatic scorers—but he regularly takes a half step or so across the foul line. (They only turn on the lasers for leagues, so there's nothing really to stop you from taking those extra few inches, except, perhaps, *ethics*.) And if he's got a tough spare to convert, he'll go a full step or two over.

If you question him about it, he just denies that it happened. I would never cheat in a game or a sport. Why lie to yourself? If you aren't good enough at it, then either accept that you aren't or work harder.

"So where are Mom and Grandma?" I ask.

"They stayed after church for some meeting about buying new Bibles or something," he says. He gives me an ironic smile. He's about as enthused about church as I am, but he goes regularly to keep peace with my mom and his. I think they go more for the community feeling than the religion. I mean, we're spiritual, but not exactly true believers.

Dad sticks a finger in his ear and starts twisting it around to kill an itch. Then he studies the nail on that finger before looking up at me with a start.

"You're all sweaty," he says, just noticing now that I'm in running gear.

"Yeah. I've been working out all morning."

"On a Sunday?"

"Every day."

He shakes his head. "I don't know how you do it. . . . Or why."

I shrug. "Can't explain it," I say. "It's just something that I have to do."

I *can* explain it, though, but only to myself. When I'm racing, there is no place to hide from a lack of determination, no way to rationalize that I'm doing my absolute best unless I really am. My faults are right there to feel. It's all a result of how hard I've worked, or how hard I haven't.

Racing produces one significant outcome: it forces you to be honest with yourself.

Shelly Ciotti

Shelly Ciotti, 17, a senior at East Scranton High School, will certainly live for many more years. It seems highly unlikely that she will return to the Scranton area for any length of time after she breezes through Bucknell University, beginning this fall.

Born in Olyphant, she moved to Scranton just in time to begin third grade at Jefferson Elementary School. For years, she was the fastest runner and best jumper in her grade, and she once beat up two boys in the same week. In junior high school, she was captain of the girls' basketball team and a district champion in the hurdles. She did not pursue sports in high school.

She has a gift for intentionally saying stupid, punny things that make her best friend, Michael, laugh. Recently they discussed driving to Florida for spring break, but the cheap-ass friend lamented that "it would cost us three hundred dollars for gas alone."

"It's gaso*line*, genius," Shelly replied.

Rumors of Shelly's alleged sexual orientation began as early as sixth grade, when someone scrawled SHELLY IS A LESBEAN inside a stall of the boys' bathroom at Jefferson. The rumor stuck, despite no hard evidence of its truthfulness. (The rumor originated because she had shouted, "I hate boys!" in class after being teased for several days about her complete lack of breasts by Lenny DiPiazza and Jimmy Colaneri. The teasing itself had begun the day after Shelly struck out Lenny three times in a Little League game.)

In recent months, Ms. Ciotti has seemed determined to assert her heterosexuality, with only a moderate degree of success. Even Michael is left unconvinced, though he has a hard time explaining to himself why it should matter.

Shelly is a big fan of *The Honeymooners,*

I Love Lucy, and *The Andy Griffith Show,* all of which were filmed way before she was born.

Also surviving are her parents, Joseph and Joanne, and an older brother, Phillip.

Courtship Rituals Tied to
Primitive Need for Attention

I GET TO SHELLY'S HOUSE way too soon for the movie, and she's not ready. She answers the door in a T-shirt and running shorts. She's got bare feet.

"You're, like, an hour early," she says. "I was just going to take a shower."

"No problem. I'll wait."

Nobody else seems to be home, so I follow her upstairs and sit on her bed, turning on the radio, which is tuned to classic rock. I try to keep my room sort of contemporary, changing the posters once in a while at least, but hers is more like a museum of girlhood (except for the dumbbells on the floor). She's got a framed photo of a horse over her bed, a Gerry McNamara bobble-head on her dresser, and a row of dolls lined up by the window. I've never really thought of her as the doll-playing type, though.

The dumbbells are the vinyl-covered kind. Orange for the five-pounders, yellow for the eights, blue for the tens, and black for the fifteens.

She grabs some fresh clothing and steps across the hall to the bathroom. Soon there's lots of steam coming out of there, since she didn't quite shut the door all the way. I imagine her in there under the shower, lathering up, but I push that out of my head in a hurry.

Shelly thinks she knows everything about me, but how could anybody know everything about somebody else? She knows the basic things, like how I look and what makes me laugh and what gets me pissed off. She knows a lot of the inner stuff, too, like how I believe in past lives and how I want to express myself creatively in ways that go beyond writing obituaries and term papers. And she keeps secrets when I tell them to her; she's the only person in the world who knows I sometimes listen to Barry Manilow.

In the past few weeks, for the first time, she's been wanting to get closer, always rubbing my shoulders or trying to hold my hand. Now I can see her through that half-inch opening in the doorway, totally naked but not in focus.

She's either way too comfortable around me or trying to drive me wild.

She's mostly dressed when she opens the door, and she smiles when she sees that I'm staring at that space. I think she blushes a little. "Mirror gets fogged up if you shut the door tight," she says.

"I can imagine."

"Very steamy," she says, and she sort of wiggles her shoulders at me and smiles with her teeth showing.

Shelly's already been accepted at Bucknell, and with her parents' two good incomes—her dad is a banker—there'll be no problem paying for it. She says she can't wait to get on with it; high school is so lame. But she keeps hinting that we could have a lot of physical fun over the next six months before she leaves. It could probably happen right now if I reached up and grabbed her. I start to reach, but I stop.

She looks at my arm, frozen there in space. "So, did you bring any joints?" she asks.

I frown and put my arm down. "Nope. Didn't get any."

"You said you were definitely getting some on Friday."

"Yeah. But the guy stuffed them into my locker, and I didn't know it until that night."

"Is that why you wanted to get into the school yesterday?"

"Yeah."

She's disappointed. The one time we smoked a joint together—about a week ago—was one of the few times we ever made out. Down on a bench in front of the courthouse after hanging out at the Steamtown Mall.

I'll admit that she's got a nice body, maybe a bit too lean. She's the type that orders only a salad and a cranberry juice when we eat at Mother's, which is a dinery place a couple of doors down from the Observer building. (It's run by a short, round Italian guy; there's no mother to be seen.) Then she'll eat half my fries. That's okay by me. She needs 'em. She's got those taut muscles and almost no fat, even where she could use some more, if you know what I mean.

Halfway through the meal, I always ask for a second order of fries, which we share.

"Guess we should get going," she says. Then, as if responding to my earlier thought, she adds, "My parents will be home anytime now."

So we walk the six blocks to the Cultural Center, which is actually a huge old Masonic temple on North Washington, about two blocks up from the courthouse square.

Despite its size, you'd barely notice the building—there's no sign and few lights—so these films and other performances are never well attended. Several times a year, they'll bring in a traveling Broadway company or a concert that fills the main theater, but mostly it's small-time artsy stuff in the side rooms.

Tonight it's an Iranian documentary with subtitles called *The Color of Love*. We're a half hour early, so I look into the theater and see that it's empty. We step over to the refreshment stand.

Chrissy is a jolly lady with curly hair, maybe about forty, who's always here selling soda and candy bars and chips and glasses of wine. I order a can of root beer and ask her if she knows anything about tonight's movie.

"Oh, it's great," she says, making a sweeping gesture with her right hand, which is holding the soda can. "We watched it this afternoon. Very interesting." She turns slightly to face Shelly, pointing at her with the soda. "You think it's tough meeting a great guy around here, honey? Wait'll you see what it's like over there."

I reach for the soda, but she's still using it as a prop. She waves it in my direction and continues speaking to Shelly. "*This* is a good guy. You know that, don't you?"

Shelly smiles, almost a laugh. "He's all right."

"You know it." Chrissy sets the root beer down hard on the counter. "And what would you like?" she asks Shelly.

"Maybe an iced tea?"

"Sure."

I look at the can, knowing that there's no way the soda won't spray all over the place if I open it, even if I wait an hour. And I'm thirsty now, so I say, "You know, maybe I'll have iced tea instead." I don't really like iced tea much, but it's not carbonated, so it's probably safe.

We take seats in the third row. There are only eight rows of seats set up, six on each side of the center aisle. About five minutes later, an older couple comes in and sits directly in front of us. I look at Shelly and roll my eyes. She just smiles. I say, "I need to use the bathroom," which I don't, but it'll give us a chance to take a different seat. We both get up and walk out of the room.

51

The door to the men's room is normal size, but you need to put both hands on it and push hard to get it open. It has one of those massive old pneumatic hinge devices, which probably weighs fifty pounds. Inside, the urinal is also huge, this bullish porcelain thing that's ancient and yellowed.

Five more people have taken seats by the time we return to the theater, and two more hustle in just as the movie is starting. So there are eleven of us in the room, about average for a showing like this.

I turn my cell phone on after the movie, and there's a message from Tucker. I call him back.

"Kerrigan," he says, "I got some news on the drug sweep. You probably want to get in here."

"You gonna be there awhile?"

"Yeah."

I look at Shelly. I can't just leave her to walk home alone, and I don't want her knowing about this drug bust. So I tell Tucker I'll be around in twenty minutes or so.

Shelly hears that and looks disappointed. "What was that about?"

"A thing at work. They can't find some notes I made last night. I know where they are."

"Can we just stop there and then hang out more?"

"Nah. I better get you home. This could take a while."

She'd been stroking my arm during the movie and leaning into my shoulder. I'm sure she was hoping for a repeat performance on a courthouse bench.

Even if I was interested—and maybe I am—there's no way I'd enjoy it with this thing hanging over my head.

"Soon," I say, and start walking. "I promise. We'll hang out again real soon."

Let me say right here that I did make out with another girl once, the summer after sophomore year. *That* was great. But I feel relieved to be off the hook with Shelly for now.

Sometimes I don't like myself very much.

I swipe my pass card and nod to the security guard, then walk up the stairs to the newsroom. I head straight for Tucker's desk, where he's talking on the phone and taking notes. He's wearing a white shirt and a dark blue tie and has a cigarette behind his ear.

I wait until he's done talking; sounds like a report on a fire in Moosic. He hangs up and looks at me kind of questioningly.

"What?" I say.

"Your name came up."

I shake my head slowly. "About the school thing, you mean?"

"Yep."

"Why?"

"You're on the list, man."

"What list?"

"The list of alleged offenders. Michael Kerrigan, age eighteen."

I try not to swallow or look guilty, but I have to. "Why would I be on a list like that?" I ask.

Tucker looks around and starts drumming on his desk with his fingers. He lowers his voice and waves me closer to him. "I could get in big-time trouble for telling you this. They said they found pot in your locker. That surprise you?"

Frickin' Joey. I start thinking hard and stay quiet.

Tucker lets out a short, huffy laugh. "Dumb move, Mike."

"It ain't mine."

"But you knew it was there?"

I take a good look around. Nobody's nearby. "I *didn't* know. Some guy put it there, and I didn't find out until Friday night."

"He just happened to put it in your locker?"

"He says he needed a place to stash it for five minutes, then forgot it was there."

Tucker smirks. "You buying that?"

"The guy's an idiot."

"So you gonna turn him in?"

I let out my breath and say, "Shit!"

The newsroom is very empty on Sunday nights—a couple of sports guys, Tucker, and a handful of editors.

"He a friend of yours?" Tucker asks.

"Sort of. Yeah. Is *his* name on the list? Joey Onager?"

"I can't tell you that."

"Shit. Do you know how much they found?"

"In your locker, you mean?"

"Yeah."

Tucker looks me over good. I suppose he'd get fired if anybody knew what he'd already told me. Probably get in some legal trouble, too. But he tells me more anyway.

"Four joints. In a plastic bag."

"That's not much," I say.

"It's enough, isn't it?"

"You think I'll get expelled?"

"Don't know. Guess it depends how convincing you are."

"About what?"

He raises his eyebrows. "Your *innocence*. Remember?"

"Yeah," I say. "My innocence."

"And how good a friend you want to be to this guy you say planted the stuff."

"Right."

"You might want to talk to a lawyer," Tucker says.

I nod slowly.

I am in very deep shit.

Catherine Kerrigan

Catherine Kerrigan of East Scranton, 47, is still very much alive. Her husband is Thomas Kerrigan, Ph.D. They will celebrate their twenty-fourth wedding anniversary in August.

Born in Hackensack, N.J., daughter of the late Henry and Roberta DeAngelo, she is a graduate of Marywood University and was previously employed by Tiny Tots preschool in Dunmore. She is a successful poet, with her work appearing in such publications as *Riverview, Happenings Magazine,* and *The East Scranton Almanac.*

She is devoted to her only son, Michael,

but shares much of her husband's somewhat clueless, detached style of parenting. Arriving home after 3:00 one recent morning, Michael stumbled into the living room to find his mother on the couch. She observed a strong odor of alcohol and asked if the friends he'd been out with had been drinking. Michael admitted that they had. "Well, I'm just glad that you weren't," she said.

Mrs. Kerrigan is a parishioner of Saint Anthony's R.C. Church. She is a member of the Scranton Historical Society and the Northeast Poets Association, and she once served as vice president of the Jefferson Elementary School PTA. She is an excellent cook but has tended in her later years to just heat up Stouffer's frozen dinners.

Study Connects Denial
to Suppressed Guilt

I WALK THE COLD STREETS for an hour before going home, and by the time I get there, my dad has gone to bed. But Mom is watching the news on CNN. She calls hello as I come into the hallway.

"Hey," I answer.

I sit on the edge of the couch and stare at the TV for a few seconds. Mom's wearing plaid pajama pants and a University of Scranton sweatshirt. Her hair—which she dyes a sort of reddish brown to hide the gray—is pulled back in a ponytail. She has a half glass of red wine sitting on the end table next to her.

It's cheap wine; they buy it by the gallon and ration it out. Mom's the type that will drive over to Dickson City to buy groceries if she sees that cans of tuna fish are five cents cheaper. She knows that it costs more than the savings just to drive over there. "It's the principle," she says.

"How was the film?" she asks.

"Pretty good."

"And did Shelly like it?"

"Seemed to."

"Did you get a bite to eat?"

"Not really. Just a drink."

Mom turns toward me and crosses one ankle over the other. She squints at me a bit and gives a half smile. "So what's wrong?" she asks.

"What do you mean?"

"I can tell. Something happen between you and Shelly?"

"No. Shelly's fine."

"Yes, but are you?"

I shrug. "I guess. Just thinking, you know?"

She looks at my face. "You seem a little shaken. Or am I imagining that?"

"Nothing shakes me." I smile. "No. I was just trying to figure something out."

"About you and Shelly?"

I roll my eyes and look down at the carpet. It's an ugly blue-green. My parents are very big on carpet—every room in the house is covered. Even the stairs are carpeted. And most of it isn't tacked down very well.

Mom is always prodding me about Shelly, subtly trying to figure out if we have sex. I'm still making up my mind about whether that's going to happen. I can't help thinking that Shelly's still trying to figure out which way she's leaning, and I don't want to be the deciding factor one way or the other.

It would probably be a relief to my mom if we did. Trying to find out if I'm interested in girls has been a recurring theme of hers since I hit puberty.

I am, by the way.

So I tell her not to worry, everything's cool. She believes me, I guess. It's true that she can usually tell when something's eating at me, but less true that she could help me with it. Both of my parents have always seemed a little stunned; every exchange between us is awkward, and we're never quite sure what the other one is driving at. They seem to think that they can be subtle and leave things unsaid but understood. Maybe that works with other poets or professors, but it leaves me with a lot to figure out for myself. I've done pretty well, but the parental-guidance thing is understated here, to say the least.

They assume I'll come to them with my problems, if I ever have any. Big assumption. And false.

I did ask her. We were walking home after watching a basketball game recently—we'd gotten hammered by Carbondale—and I said right straight out, "Are you gay?"

Shelly laughed sort of nervously. "I don't know." She stopped and put her arms around me and pressed her chest hard into mine (we were both wearing coats), got up on her toes, and kissed me on the lips for about six seconds. Then she reached around and grabbed my butt. "Not tonight, I'm not."

So we ducked around the side of an abandoned building and made out on a stoop for maybe fifteen minutes. It was about twenty degrees, and some of our saliva started to freeze on my chin.

We went back to her house and talked to her parents for a few minutes, then they both yawned and said they were tired and went upstairs, obviously to give us some privacy (but not too much). By then, the mood had passed (at least on my end), so we turned on the TV but just left it on whatever channel it was tuned to and talked about "our futures."

"School is so frickin' boring," she said. "Can't you just not wait until we get the heck out of here?"

"Yeah," I replied, trying to sound more enthusiastic than I felt.

"What?" she asked, picking up on my halfhearted tone. "You actually like it here?"

"It's not *so* bad," I said. "I don't even know where I'm going yet." Shelly's already at Bucknell in her head; this is just a last long visit home. I'm still very much here. "I don't hate it."

"I don't *hate* it either," she said. "But, my God, that basketball game tonight was the highlight of my week. How pathetic is that?"

We stared at the TV. And then I realized that her eagerness to flee this place was part of the problem I was having with her. Sometimes when I can't wait to just get the hell out of Scranton—get to some college far away and then find a job in California or Boston and only come home for Christmas—sometimes then I get to feeling guilty. Like somehow by leaving I'd be turning my back on home and letting it decay even further. Like I should be doing something to make this city great again instead of fleeing.

And that's about the same reason I'm not so quick to jump into bed with her. We pretty much grew up together—we used to play board games every day after school; then we got to junior high and talked each other into going out for track; and we went to a couple of dances together, but we never danced and spent most of the evening laughing at how klutzy the boys who tried to were. I don't want that capped off with a few months of sex and then it's over. Use me up and never look back. If that sounds like I'm some prude or a wimp, then I guess I have to accept that.

I don't tell her any of this.

"And I'm *not* gay," she said. "I mean, we all fall somewhere along a sexual spectrum. I'm not saying I'm in the dead center, but I know I'm not one extreme or the other. Where the heck are *you*?"

"I'm *straight*. What do you think?"

She shrugged. "You seem kind of reluctant."

"With *you* I am."

She folded her arms and leaned back on the couch. "Thanks a lot."

"It's not—" I lower my voice to a whisper, remembering her parents upstairs. "It's not—you're great."

She gave me a smirk and stuck out her tongue. "Then kiss me," she said. And I did. For quite a while. It felt good. I relaxed.

But I was pissed off at myself the next morning.

Joseph Onager

Joseph Onager, 18, a lifelong resident of Scranton, isn't dead yet. A senior at East Scranton High School, he may or may not graduate in June, but it won't make much difference anyway. With or without the diploma, he will likely wind up as a laborer and continue living at home with his parents.

Joseph was a decent shortstop in the East Scranton Little League and later developed an interest in bowling. Friends recall that he used to collect interesting stones and pebbles and that he sang a brief solo during the fourth-grade holiday concert at Jefferson Elementary School.

He worked last summer as a dishwasher at Carmella's Italian Restaurant, and in recent months he has been employed as a low-level drug runner for an outfit in South Scranton.

Also surviving are his abusive parents, Gustavo and Ellen, who appear to be absent even when they are present.

SECTION C
SPORTS

Costly Fumble Threatens Season

I'VE BEEN IN A COLD SWEAT most of the morning and not even trying to pay attention in my classes. I know I'll be getting called to the principal's office anytime now. Nobody's said anything, so it looks like this is all still confidential. But it's bound to explode soon.

I run into Jay in the hallway, and he raises his fist. "Ker-ri-gan," he says. "Practice starts Wednesday, man. Be ready to kick some butt."

I nod and swallow hard. I should have adrenaline pumping through me, uplifted by Jay's enthusiasm and the knowledge that big things are going to happen soon on the track. But it's not looking so good right now.

"I'm psyched," Jay says. "It's like our whole career has built to this season, you know? It's gonna be awesome."

"Yeah," I say. "It is."

I see Joey at lunch, and he waves me over. He's at the end of one of the long tables by himself. I have no appetite, so I just grab an orange juice and some chocolate-chip cookies and sit next to him.

"You in the clear?" he asks.

I shrug. "Doubt it," I say, but I suppose there's a tiny chance that they'll leave me alone.

"Nothing happened yet?"

I shake my head.

"I would have thought if they were going to haul you in, they'd have done it first thing this morning."

"You would have thought." I push away the juice; no way I can stomach anything. "You hear about anybody else?"

"Nothing yet," he says.

But I don't think it'll be long. I can see the vice principal, Mr. Peterson, looking at us from across the lunchroom with his crew cut and running-back build, and I think he's making sure we don't leave. Maybe they've got Joey tied up in this now, too. Who knows? That would certainly ease things for me if they nailed him on their own without any word from me.

Joey sees Peterson staring at us and says, "Here it comes." But he drops the tough-guy persona right away and whispers to me urgently, "I swear to God, Mike, I'm never trafficking again."

"Right," I say. You don't just walk away from something like that.

"No way. I was scared shitless all weekend. Don't turn me in, man. I'll owe you big-time."

This doesn't surprise me. All Joey's drug business and partying and hanging out all night is a front. He's basically a poser without much happening. He does that stuff to try to impress the world that he's got something going on, but he doesn't.

"So I'm supposed to just take whatever they throw at me?" I ask. "I get kicked out of school to cover your sorry ass?"

He cranes his neck and looks at the ceiling, then turns to me. There's fear in his eyes. I see him swallow hard. "They'd eat me alive," he says. "My parents would kill me. I mean *kill*. And the school would be glad to see me hang."

I know he's right. His mom smacked him around in front of me plenty of times when we were younger. And he must have got worse from his father in private. Joey gets a bad deal from teachers, too, even though he asks for a lot of it with his attitude.

Peterson is walking toward us now. He's looking straight at Joey, who sits up but looks away.

Peterson puts his hand on my shoulder and says, "We need to have a talk," but he's still staring at Joey.

"Now?" I say.

"Yeah. Now."

I push the two cookies toward Joey and say, "Help yourself."

Joey says, "Thanks."

Peterson is standing there. He speaks to Joey. "So, Mr. Onager. How are you?"

Joey looks up at him blankly. "Okay."

"I'm taking your friend for a little chat with Mrs. Davis," Peterson says. "Maybe you know what it's about."

Joey shakes his head and frowns. "How would I know that?"

Peterson gives a menacing kind of shrug. "You guys are buddies. Maybe you could help him out."

"I don't know what you're talking about."

"Well, maybe you should think about it," Peterson says. "I'm just thinking you might be able to spare your good friend a lot of trouble. But maybe I'm wrong."

"Sounds wrong to me."

"Well, you think about it," Peterson says. "Meantime, Mike and I will go have our talk with the principal. Maybe I'll see you later."

I stand and follow Peterson out of the lunchroom. When we reach the hallway, I ask, "What's this about?"

He turns to me and gives a smirk. "Anything missing from your locker this morning?"

"Not that I know of."

"That's strange," he says, "because we found an interesting package there over the weekend."

I just keep walking. When we're a few feet from the principal's office, he stops.

"Listen, Kerrigan," he whispers through his teeth, "you can play dumb if you want, but there's a detective waiting in here, and we've got pretty strong evidence against you. You can be honest, or you can get squeezed until you squirm. Make it easy on yourself, bud. I know you're not dealing, but you know who is."

"No, I don't," I say.

He raises his eyebrows. "You and your lunch buddy are sharing more than cookies, Mike. He'll be dead meat one of these days. The sooner, the better. For you *and* me."

The meeting with the detective and the principal went something like this:

"How did the drugs get in your locker?"

"Somebody must have put them there."

"And that somebody wasn't you?"

"No. It wasn't."

"But you must have some idea who would put them there."

I shrugged. "Could have been a lot of people."

"Why would a lot of people have the idea to put marijuana in your locker?"

"They wouldn't."

73

"But somebody did."

"Obviously."

"Well, unless you think you know who it was, we can only assume that you're lying."

"About what?"

"About how it got there."

"You mean, if I can't say who put the stuff there, then it must have been me all along?"

"You can see how one would reach that conclusion."

We kept going around like that, but I didn't budge. I know the facts: Joey was trafficking drugs, and he'll probably get nailed someday, but I'll get hit with possession whether I turn him in or not.

So I've been suspended from school, and it's likely to get worse. What they want to do is kick me out permanently as an example, but they'll get over it and let me back if I turn in my dealer. Thing is, I don't even know who the "dealer" is. Joey is just the delivery guy. But I think they'd be satisfied if I gave them his name. Then they could pressure him the same way to lead them up the chain.

Going to jail is very unlikely, but I'm sure I'll get some kind of fine and probation. I'm more worried about getting expelled. That means no graduation, no track season, no college. So if I do the easy thing and rat on Joey, my life can be relatively normal within a couple of weeks. If I protect him, I'm pretty well screwed out of everything.

For now, I'm not saying a word. But in my head, I'm trying to figure who to blame for all this. Joey put that shit in my locker. That's indisputable. So he carries a lot of the responsibility. All I told him was that I wanted a few joints and I'd pick them up from him sometime last weekend. I never said anything about dropping them off in my locker. As far as I can see, they were his until I took possession, which I never did.

Here's some irony. Assuming that I keep my mouth shut and he stays out of trouble, Joey will graduate in June and I won't.

I have to say that I'm not all that happy with Shelly either. She's the reason I decided to buy the dope in the first place. You could almost say that I'm the victim.

Anyway, I can make things a whole lot better for myself by playing along with the system and telling them where the pot came from.

But I know better than that. I ordered the drugs. Nobody made me do it.

I have until noon tomorrow to come clean or get expelled.

Both of my parents are waiting at the kitchen table when I get there. I say hello.

"The principal called," Mom says evenly.

"I figured she would."

"So what's the story?" Dad asks. "They say you know who put the drugs there."

"I didn't say that."

"I know you didn't. But they insist that you must know."

"They can be wrong."

"Are they?"

I scratch my head and lean against the counter. "*They* don't know the answer to that."

Dad's tone heats up a little. "But do *you*?"

"Maybe I do. But I don't like them just assuming that I'm lying to them."

"But their assumption is correct in this case?"

I don't say anything. Dad lets out his breath in a huff.

"Michael," Mom says, "if you tell the truth, you'll minimize the trouble for yourself. If you choose *not* to, then the consequences are looking pretty harsh."

"I *know* that, Mom. You think I don't know that?"

"Yes, I know that you do. But I don't understand why you think you need to protect someone who's put you in such serious jeopardy."

Dad pipes in. "You haven't been threatened, have you?"

"By who?"

"By whoever planted the drugs."

"No," I say scornfully. "Nobody threatened me with anything except the cop and the principal. Screw them anyway."

My dad shakes his head slowly. "I think you're the one who's screwed, Sport. And you can get yourself out of it very easily. Tell the truth about who got you in trouble and get on with your life. It would be ridiculous for you to take the fall while some drug dealer walks free."

"You haven't done anything wrong," Mom says.

I stand there and stare at them, not sure what to say. Like I figured, they believe that I'm innocent.

I suppose that should make me feel good. They have faith in me.

Does that make them supportive or stupid?

Star Prospect Sent Packing

I PUT ON A WHITE SHIRT and a maroon tie and go to work twenty minutes early, mostly because I want to see what's up. I've never worn a tie here before, but maybe this is a good day for it. Tucker isn't around. I ask if he's been in and am told that he's in the managing editor's office.

Tucker wouldn't usually work on a Monday, but I figured he'd be here because of the drug bust. It's his story; he'd want to follow it even on a day off.

I see Larry staring at me from the sports department. I nod and walk over. He's wearing a T-shirt that says HELP WANTED: *Many Positions Available*. Under the words are cartoony drawings of people in various sexual positions. Great office attire.

I glance at the old Gerry McNamara poster, showing

his classic jump-shooting form. The pride of Scranton. Undeniable.

"So what's new?" Larry asks sarcastically, as if he already knows. He probably does know. Everybody in the newsroom probably does. Maybe I'm paranoid, but I don't seem to be getting the usual warm greetings from people.

"Not much," I say.

"Oh no?" He's giving me a half sneer, like he's disgusted with my behavior. He's got a real case. The guy is drunk most of the time, even at work, so how is this different? Like there's some sacred newsroom trust against smoking dope? And suddenly this sleazy sports guy is Mr. Morality.

I see Tucker come out of the office and head for his desk. Larry is looking over that way, too, as Greg, the managing editor, comes out and looks around.

"Nice knowing ya," Larry says, looking away from me and back at the computer screen. "Don't let the door hit you in the ass on the way out."

"Yeah, screw you, too," I say.

He gives a dismissive laugh. "Good riddance."

Greg catches my eye and motions for me to come to his office. He's young to be running a news department—maybe thirty-five, neat haircut, wears a suit.

"Why don't you shut the door?" he says as I come in.

So I shut it.

"I'm sure you know that we'll be publishing a story on the drug sweep either tomorrow or Wednesday," he says.

"Sure."

"Under the circumstances, it's best that you not work tonight. Understand?"

"Yeah."

"You're an adult, so you'll be named in the article unless the charges are suddenly dropped," he says. "That's our policy in situations like this. If you're eighteen, we run your name."

"I know. I figured that."

I haven't even sat down. But I guess that's it. "So I should go?"

"I'm afraid so," he says.

"What about Friday?"

He thinks for a second, maybe not sure what I meant.

"I'm scheduled to work," I say.

"Oh," he finally says. "We'll call you."

I reach for the doorknob.

"I'll walk you out," he says.

So he escorts me through the newsroom and down the stairs to the employee entrance. Totally unnecessary— I would have just left on my own—but I guess I understand. You can't have dangerous criminals hanging around.

"Mike," he says as we reach the door, "I have to take your pass card. Just while we sort things out."

"What for?" I ask. They really are treating me like a criminal.

"Company policy," he says.

"Company policy." I take the pass card out of my wallet and hand it over.

"Good luck with this thing," Greg says. He lowers his voice and leans closer. "I heard you can get the charges dropped and be reinstated at school if you come clean about the dealer."

"That's what they tell me."

He looks a little surprised. If I know that, why haven't I done it, right? He seems reluctant to kick me out. "You've been doing a good job here," he says.

"Thanks," I say, but I'm squirming and looking toward the street.

"I hope it can continue," he says. He squeezes my arm. "Don't be a martyr."

"Right," I say. "I'll see ya."

I walk a few blocks and sit on a bench at the courthouse square, staring up at the ancient Electric City neon sign atop a nearby building. I feel numb, like maybe this isn't really happening. But it is.

I reach into my pocket for my cell phone and punch in Shelly's number.

"Where've you been?" she asks instead of saying hello. "I tried calling you a million times."

"I shut off my phone. You heard what happened?"

"Duh. Of course I heard. Where are you?"

"Downtown."

"Are you all right?"

"Yeah."

I fill her in on the suspension and the pressure and all that. I hate talking on the phone, though, so I tell her I'll come get her. "Your mom hear about this?" I ask.

"Yeah. But she also heard you got set up."

"I didn't get set up."

"You know what I mean," she says. "It's not what it looks like."

"Why does everybody think that?"

"I guess they just can't believe you'd be guilty."

"I guess I can't believe it myself."

She opens her front door before I'm up the walk. She must have been watching for me.

We walk up the hill and right back toward the courthouse. After we turn the corner, she stops and puts her hand on the back of my neck. It's still cold out; she's wearing big blue mittens, and the warmth she generates is both internal and external. Very soothing.

"This has to be killing you," she says. "I know you want to protect Joey, but look what you're letting happen to you."

"How do you know it's Joey?"

"Come on," she says, touching my face. "It's *so* obvious to anybody who knows you guys."

"That he sells drugs?"

"Doesn't he?"

I start walking again. "He did me a favor. He *screwed up* the favor big-time. But I asked him to get me the dope. He was dumb enough to put it in my locker, but it was my stuff. Or it was about to be, anyway."

We take a seat on the same bench where we made out one time, and she leans tight against me, gripping my hand. I let out my breath and we just sit there, and I start to relax just a little bit again. I appreciate her being here; it makes me feel like I'm not totally alone with this problem. Not much she can do to resolve it, but it helps to have somebody actually listen.

"You can't let yourself get expelled," she says.

"Dealers get jail time," I say.

"You're not a dealer."

"I didn't say I was. What they want from me is a statement about who *is*. I don't even know if Joey's been dealing. I just know he knows where to get it."

"Everybody in school knows places where they can get it, don't they?"

I shrug. "Probably. But Joey's very small-time. Like I said, he was just doing me a favor."

We're quiet for several minutes. She's caressing my fingers.

"Shit," I say softly.

"What?"

"Nothing. Just this whole thing sucks. I shouldn't be in this much trouble, but if I get myself out of it, then Joey gets way more trouble than he deserves."

"But you can't take the blame for everything," she says.

"You don't graduate, you don't go to college, your reputation goes to hell. You have to think about all that."

I laugh, even though this isn't funny. "I got sent home from work, too, you know. This all gets reported in the paper. They'll probably fire me."

A police car drives by, and I hunch down a little, even though we've got every right to be here. But I feel watched, and I know that everywhere I go now, I'll feel like people are suspicious of me.

"When I was twelve, me and Joey went into a convenience store and stole about six candy bars," I say. "Joey's got this crappy old pair of shorts on, and on the way out, the bars slip through a hole in his pocket and land on the floor. The clerk sees it and yells at him to stop, which he does, but I'm already out the door, and I run like hell up to the park and hide out. The clerk gets Joey's name and calls his parents, but he won't give up my name, so I get off free. The next day, I see Joey and he's got welts on his arms and under his eye. But he says just to forget it."

"Is *that* why you're protecting him?" she asks, as if there's no parallel at all.

"Not exactly," I say. "But we were always doing things like that—throwing rocks through factory windows at night or stealing bottles of soda—and I always seemed to get away with it. He usually did, too, but he got caught a few times and never ratted on me."

She gives me a very surprised look, like she can't believe I'd really do anything criminal.

"We grew *up*," I say. "I was twelve!"

"God," she says, shaking her head.

"Anyway," I say, "I still don't know if I *am* going to protect him. I have until tomorrow afternoon to decide."

"You can't compare stealing Hershey bars with selling drugs, Mike."

"There's more to it than that," I say. "This isn't even about protecting him, you know. I don't want him getting arrested, but that's only part of it. Everybody keeps telling me to tell the truth, but they're all full of shit. They have this preconceived notion of what they think the truth is. But they're wrong."

"So make it right."

"This is about honesty, Shelly."

"Honesty means telling the truth, Mike. Doesn't it?"

I stare at the sidewalk, then start nodding my head slowly. "That's exactly what it's about," I say.

Decisive Match Is a No-brainer

It's STILL EARLY when I walk Shelly home. She leans into me at the doorway and kisses my forehead lightly. "I know you'll make the right decision," she says, sounding like my mom.

I just shrug. I don't know what I'm doing. I need a run. But first I need to go see Joey. I don't know if I'm going there to talk things out or to beat him up, but I'm going. Somehow that will help me decide.

"See ya," I say. Shelly watches me from the step until I'm out of sight; I keep looking back, and she keeps standing there.

So I walk up the hill and through the downtown and over to Joey's. They live in one of those big old Victorians on Myrtle; I think it was passed down to them from Joey's father's family.

I used to come over here once in a while after school. One time me and Joey went up to the attic and crawled out on the roof, which is steep and fairly high. We could see way over to the valley and, much closer, into people's yards and windows.

We were about thirteen, and one of the neighbors started yelling at us to get the heck down from there before we fell and broke our necks or worse. Joey just laughed. "I fall off here all the time," he called back, which was totally untrue, of course. We *would* have broken our necks or worse if we fell.

The neighbor called the cops, and a car came by. The officer got out and looked up at us with his hands on his hips and said, "You boys all right?"

"No problem," Joey said.

"You better get down. You're making people nervous."

Joey looked at me with a smile. "That's good," he said, loud enough for the cop to hear.

We crawled back into the attic and went to the kitchen and ate peanut butter sandwiches.

Mr. Onager opens the door and greets me enthusiastically. He's wearing old gray pants; a white T-shirt is stretched over his huge stomach. His hair, which is receding and thin, is sticking up as if he's been lying on the couch.

"Come in, Mike. Come in," he says, smiling and sweeping his arm toward the living room. So I follow him in. You never know what he'll be like: sometimes he's funny and engaging; sometimes he's practically brain-dead and nasty.

"Let me make you some room," he says, picking up a pile of seven or eight old Bibles from an armchair and setting them on the floor. He brushes the chair with his hand and motions for me to sit.

"Joey ain't home," he says. "You thirsty? Want a beer or something? A soda?"

"Sure," I say. "Soda. Whatever you got."

He goes over to the kitchen. There's a big stack of hunting and fishing magazines on the floor in front of the sofa, and old papers—postcards, ledgers, letters—on the coffee table. Everything's dark in here—the old upholstered chairs, the ornate wooden tables, the wallpaper, the hardwood floors. I think things have stayed pretty much the same for three or four generations of Onagers. I pick up one of the postcards showing downtown Scranton. The postmark on the back is 1916.

He comes back and hands me a can of Sam's Club orange soda. "I just got all that crap at an auction," he says. "Cool, huh?"

"Yeah," I say, picking up another postcard showing the Jermyn Hotel in 1925.

"I don't know," he says. "Most people would just burn that stuff. I think it's interesting. Lives lived, you know?"

"Definitely."

"I don't know where the hell he is," he says, meaning Joey.

I glance down at the Bibles. "You studying these?"

He laughs. "Nah. I got the whole bunch of 'em for two bucks, and I couldn't resist." He seems a little embarrassed. He explains, "I hate to see stuff like that get chucked, you know? It's got deepness or something. Etern— What's the word? Eternality? You know what I mean."

"Sure. Stuff has meaning," I say. "Believe me. You know these obituaries I write? You talk to the families, and it's always something simple that they remember most about the one who died. Their cookbooks or their bottle collection or the scarves they knitted for their grandchildren."

"Yeah," he says, "that's what I mean. We got shit in the attic here—my old man's army medals, *his* old man's tools, my grandmother's buttons and sewing needles. I could never throw that stuff away. Haven't even looked at it in years. . . . I ought to."

He sits back on the couch and burps. "Scuse me," he says. "You hungry? The wife's at some church thing, and God knows where Joey's at. I got a stew cooking."

"Yeah, I can smell it. Smells good."

"I tell ya, I got this nice lean pork, browned it up in olive oil, threw in a bunch of spices . . . nothing hot, just parsley and garlic and something else—black pepper—and it's been simmering for about three hours. The key is a bottle of beer—domestic stuff. If you use Heineken or Molson or something imported like that, it gets sour. I use Stegmaier; they brew it right over in Wilkes-Barre, you know. Anyway, you simmer that all together, and my God— you can smell it, can't ya?"

"Yeah. It's ready?"

"It's ready. Oh, and a little can of tomato paste. You'll see."

He goes back to the kitchen. I get the impression that he doesn't work much. He always seems to be on call to do some sort of labor, but the calls don't come in very often.

I figure Mrs. Onager is out at some bar. It's after ten; I don't see any church events going on this late. Maybe Mr. Onager is lonely. He sure seems glad to have company.

He comes in with two bowls of the stew and hands one to me. "Joey should be eating this," he says. "He's out every friggin' night."

I dig into the stew, which is fantastic.

"I can be a prick," he says, acknowledging, I suppose, why his son and wife are missing. He laughs. "So how are you?"

I don't even hesitate. "I'm in trouble."

"Aren't we always? Hey, you want bread?"

"Yeah. Why not."

"I got some great bread." He moves some of the post-cards and stuff and sets his bowl on the coffee table, then quickly gets a couple of hunks of sourdough bread for us.

"Sop up that gravy," he says. "It's the best part."

He clicks on the TV and switches to one of the sports

channels, where two obscure middleweights are boxing. "You a fight fan?" he asks.

"Sure. I watch some."

"Idiots beating each other's brains out," he says with a laugh. He looks over at me. "Firsthand experience. I know."

"You fought?"

"Right here in Scranton mostly. I won a few fights. Long time ago."

"Wow," I say. "You fight anybody good?"

He shakes his head. "Nah. We were all bums."

His face brightens. "Tell you what, though. I ran into Muhammad Ali once in New York. In an elevator at Madison Square Garden. Larger than life.

"Funny, bright. The guy just glowed. I was in his presence for what, maybe eighteen seconds? But I never forgot that feeling. The guy was the greatest. So quick. Brilliant in the ring. I saw him fight in person once. . . . Never been another one like him. He stayed true to his heart, you know what I mean?"

"I guess. Yeah. . . . So why'd you stop?"

"Ah," he says, giving a wave of his hand. "I had maybe ten fights. Eleven, actually. I won five times and had two draws. I only got knocked out that one time. My last fight. I didn't *know* it was going to be my last fight, but it was."

He takes a bite of the gravy-soaked bread and continues talking with his mouth full. "Six-round fight. We're in the fifth. Pretty close. I take a right hand to the temple so friggin' hard you wouldn't believe it."

He swallows and wipes some crumbs from his mouth with the back of his hand. "I was only out for maybe five seconds, but that was it. It screwed my brain. After, I'm sitting in the locker room, and I can't stop crying. I don't even know why. I'm not sad about losing the fight or nothing; it ain't that. I'm just shook up. Like I just faced death, maybe. I cried for an hour and a half.

"Anyway, I didn't think I was quitting. I went back to the gym to train, but I never had the desire anymore. I recovered physically from the knockout, don't get me wrong, but I never recovered as an *athlete*, you get me? I took that one good punch, and it finished me."

He leans back and smiles.

"Amazing," I say.

He shrugs. "Omar Medina," he says. "That was the guy's name. From Harrisburg. . . . I've never hit a living soul since.

"Anyway," he says, scraping some pork from his front teeth with his fingernail, "what's the trouble you mentioned?"

"Just some shit at school," I say. "I, uh, did some stuff. Kind of illegal."

He rolls his eyes. "Tell me about it," he says, but he doesn't mean it. That just means that we all do things we regret.

We sit quietly for a minute, me thinking about my trouble and him thinking who knows what.

He jabs a finger into the air toward me, and his eyes get wider, as if he's got a big idea to share. "Onions," he says. "I didn't mention them. You should brown some chopped onions with the meat. You have to. It *makes* the stew."

I laugh. "Will do."

"You'll make this recipe?"

"I will. I definitely will."

"I could write it down," he says. He stands and picks up his bowl. "You want more?"

"No. But thanks. It was great."

"It's a huge pot." He takes my bowl and keeps talking as he makes his way to the kitchen. "I still got it simmering; the longer, the better. When Joey ever gets the hell home, he can have some. The kid's too scrawny; he needs to eat."

Mr. Onager wants me to stay at least until the boxing match is over, but I tell him I'm tired and I need to go for a run to sort some things out in my head. He scribbles down the recipe on the back of an envelope, and I stick it in my wallet and walk out and down the hill.

From a certain spot on Jefferson, I can see the institutions that have given me opportunities and now have taken them away. Over to my left about four blocks and down the hill, I can just make out the tip of the top of East Scranton High School. Nearly straight ahead, all the way across downtown, is the Observer building, one of the few that are lit up this late on a Monday evening. And behind me and a couple of blocks over (I can't quite see it) is our house.

Maybe I'm more like this city than I thought. Not just

the resilience but the continual mistakes. I've just taken several big steps backward, and I'm on the verge of several more. Can I then move forward fast enough to wind up ahead of the game?

I took that one good punch, and it finished me. That's not something I'd want to be telling people thirty years from now.

I've got too much invested in myself to let that happen.

SECTION D

BUSINESS and
CLASSIFIEDS

Downtown Renewal Plans
Still Unclear

No DECISION YET, just a cold gnawing feeling in my gut and the back of my head. I'm waiting a few more minutes to start my run, until midnight. That's symbolic, I guess, but of what I don't know. The opposite of high noon, I suppose, the hour when my decision is due.

I'll cover my safest nighttime route, basically sticking to the roads on the perimeter of the downtown business area. Plenty of streetlights, even though the city is mostly sleeping.

There's an icy wind now, but I don't care. I run the loop easy, along Jefferson to Vine, down past Lackawanna Junior College and the Cultural Center, over past the Observer building, then left one block to Lackawanna Avenue and past Quint's Army-Navy store and under the overpass outside the Steamtown Mall, beyond the Coney Island Lunch and back up toward the Radisson Hotel. Each loop is a little over two miles. I pick up the pace on the second one and really tear through the quiet streets, feeling the pressure of other runners on my heels, chasing me but never overtaking me.

It feels like midrace, when you're pushing the pace and daring anyone to follow, knowing that you've got plenty left for a devastating kick that will leave them staggering in your wake. For now, it's a determined, steady drive.

You get in this flow, almost like a trance. I'm in that state now: smooth, fast, deliberate.

And instead of making the left on Vine, I keep going and work my way over to Woodlawn and make the sharp uphill right. I'm tired, and this is the longest, steepest hill in Scranton, but I'm running purely on emotion now, ready to test myself. We'll see how tough I am.

I've quit before in races and in workouts and in other ways, letting myself down any number of times. Losing races I know I could have won if I'd been a little bit gutsier, less afraid of the pain. Or if I'd been less afraid of failure instead of taking the easy way and finishing second or third when the other options were to go for broke and win or go for broke and break, finish fifth or eighth or last but at least knowing that I'd gone for it.

This hill is insanely steep. My quads weigh a ton.

No more playing it safe. I'm running to win this season.

No more rationalizing. No more thinking that second best is almost as good as first.

My shoulders and thighs are burning, and I can taste that stew starting to repeat on me, not digested yet, ready to come back up. I've only covered a couple of blocks of the hill, but suddenly I can't run another step. I slow to nearly a walk and stretch my arms over my head. Then I stop.

So maybe I'm not as tough as I thought.

But it's been a long couple of days. I'm exhausted physically and emotionally. I can lie and get off clean or tell the truth and be screwed out of everything. I'm sweating but feel suddenly cold; the wind is biting my face. I should walk back home, get some sleep. Give myself a break and get this over with in the morning. Start out fresh and be at track practice on Wednesday afternoon. Get my job back. Get tight with Shelly. Be the best I can be.

I walk to the bottom of the hill and stand on the corner. It wouldn't be fair for me to miss the most important sports season of my life so far. It's not fair that I've worked so hard all winter, that I'm in prime condition and ready for more, and yet I'm putting myself in danger of missing out because sleazy little Joey doesn't deserve what he'd get if I saved my own butt. Too bad. I've worked too hard. I want it too bad. I've got too much at stake this season. My last high school track season.

I think back to another final season.

Things were never quite as great for Syracuse after that championship run when Gerry McNamara was a freshman.

And in his senior year, things hit a low point. They were only the ninth seed in the Big East Conference tournament, and it looked like his career was going to end on a sour note.

But he nailed a last-second three-pointer in the first round to beat Cincinnati by one, then hit another to force overtime in the quarterfinals against Connecticut. Syracuse won that game, too. Connecticut was ranked number one in the nation at that point.

In the semis, Syracuse came from fifteen points behind to upset Georgetown—with the fans at Madison Square Garden chanting, "GER-ry, GER-ry" through the entire game. Then they beat Pitt in the final. Needless to say, McNamara was named the tournament's MVP. And again, everybody in Scranton felt like they were a part of it.

They lost in the first round of the NCAA tournament the following week. But McNamara had cemented his legend. We'll be talking about him around here forever.

My heart is pumping hard, and I feel the sweat turning cold on my face. I feel the heat in my legs and the hard, steady pumping of my lungs. I taste Mr. Onager's stew, but I also hear his words again, and they are at least as chilling as the wind: *I never recovered as an athlete, you get me? I took that one good punch, and it finished me.*

Here's a race where I quit on myself. District track championships last spring, seeded section of the 800 meters. I'm seeded sixth, but I've been coming on strong lately, and my coach tells me I can win. What I have to do is take it out hard and rob the favorite of his kick. Make sure he has nothing left for the final straightaway.

So I go out fast for the first lap, coming through in fifty-eight seconds with him right on my butt. I lead through the first turn of the second lap, still pushing hard and feeling good. But I hit the backstretch and my mind starts taking over, telling me to ease up a bit so I'll be able to finish fast.

Exactly what my coach told me not to do. *When it hurts the most, start pushing harder*, he said. Do I listen? No. I try to relax, but I realize what pain I'm in. Three guys rush by me as we go into the final turn. That little rest I took is doing me no good at all; I'm tying up and dying. But I know I have it in me to stay with them, to fight back past them and win the race. But I don't. I give up. I finish fourth and tell myself I did the best I possibly could. But deep inside, I know better.

A car goes by and shakes me out of my daydream. I clench my fists and take a step toward home, then stop again and turn. No more quitting. *One good punch, and it finished me.*

I could take a thousand hard punches. I look back up the hill, shut my eyes for a second, and start running as fast as I can.

I'm dying by the time I reach Capouse, but I fight through it and battle my way up to Wyoming, churning my arms and my legs. One mouthful of puke comes up, and I spit it out hard, never breaking stride, cursing at myself to keep moving, to run even harder, to never quit on myself again!

Keep it coming, I'll just get stronger. Knock me down, and I'll get right back up. Take away the things I desire, but the desire itself won't go away.

Getting in trouble—and trying to get out of it—has one thing in common with giving up in a race. You can try to rationalize your way out of it, but the truth comes back to get you. You at least have to be honest with yourself.

Even if you decide to screw the system.

Three East Students Expelled Following Weekend Drug Bust

By TUCKER HAMMOND
Observer Staff Writer

SCRANTON—Three students were expelled from East Scranton High School on Tuesday following a weekend sweep of lockers that produced a modest amount of marijuana. Four others have been suspended.

City police lieutenant Peter O'Dell said all seven students have been charged with possession of marijuana. The three who were expelled—Frederick Pasella, 19; Lucien Douglas, 18; and Michael Kerrigan, 18—were scheduled to graduate from the school in June. The four students who were suspended are all juveniles. Their suspensions range from three to seven days.

Officials said the drug sweep was part of an ongoing program in which lockers are searched at least once each month. Principal Sonya Davis said the sweeps have been an effective deterrent against drugs in the school.

"The sweeps are unannounced, of course, but I think kids have come to expect them," Davis said. "I'm actually surprised that we found anything this weekend. The past few times, we've come up empty."

Davis said the three expelled students may be eligible to work toward general equivalency diplomas (GEDs) beginning after their class graduates in June, but they will not be readmitted to any schools in the Scranton district. Lieutenant O'Dell said charges against several other students are pending.

South Side Businessmen
Remain Active

OH YEAH. I GOT FIRED, TOO, so I've written my last obituary.

Got a letter of acceptance from Kutztown University this morning. Contingent on successful graduation from high school, of course. Not going to happen.

And track practice starts this afternoon. Coach will have to name a new captain.

I stayed in bed until after my dad left for work and Mom went to the library, just staring at the ceiling mostly. Then I got up and read the paper—I knew the drug-bust article would be there, but it still stopped me cold. I heated some leftover Chinese food in the microwave. Now I'm sitting in front of the television in the living room, watching a rerun of *Bonanza* from forty years ago.

I can hear freezing rain hitting the windows, and I get up to look outside. And I see Joey walking up the hill in the middle of the street, toward our house, hunched over in a big old brown coat, no gloves or hat.

I open the front door and wait for him. He gives me a knowing frown and walks up the steps.

"What's up?" I say.

"Nothing."

"You cut school?"

"Yeah. Everybody's giving me shit about what happened," he says. "I'll go back tomorrow."

We sit in the living room. I give him some paper towels to wipe off his hair, which is dripping from the sleet.

"You want something to eat?" I ask, but he's holding his stomach. He shakes his head.

"What happened?" I ask.

"I got beat up pretty good."

"By your dad?"

"No." He gives me a sharp look like I've got some nerve saying that. "Some of my friends from the South Side paid me a visit." He rolls his eyes. His drug connections.

"Oh."

"They told me to be sure to bring you their best wishes," he says.

"Screw them."

"They just said to keep on keeping your mouth shut and there'd be no trouble."

"Assholes."

106

Joey leans back in the chair and rubs his arm. "They said this was just a sample beating, in case I talk."

"Just stay the hell away from them."

"I plan to."

He stares at the TV screen; Ben and Hoss are confronted by some bandits, guns drawn. "My dad sent you a note," Joey says, taking a piece of paper out of his pocket.

"You told him what happened?"

"No way. But he saw your name in the paper."

"So what's the note about?"

"I have no idea."

I unfold the paper and read it aloud.

> MIKE I dint mention the carrots. Put them in when you add the beer and water. Don't peel them. And don't use those little babie carrots. Use whole carrots, washed BUT NOT PEELED. Cut off the ends.
> —Gus

"Important stuff," I say, smiling slightly.

Joey shrugs. "He's a good cook."

"Yeah, I know. He ought to get a job as a chef."

"Your girlfriend called me last night and told me I was a total scumbag for letting you hang," Joey says.

"She's not my girlfriend."

"She said if I had any guts at all, I would have fessed up and got you off the hook. . . . She's probably right."

"Probably. But it's too late now. I'm screwed."

He shrugs again. "They would have killed me."

"They didn't."

We sit there quietly for several minutes until a commercial for an online dating service comes on the screen.

"So what are you going to do?" Joey asks.

"I don't know. Get a job in a kitchen or something. My dad says I can get a GED by the end of the summer and go to Lackawanna for a semester or two, then try to transfer out. But I'll be stuck in Scranton for at least another year."

"Yeah. Me too."

I look at him, but I don't say anything. He'll be stuck here for longer than that. Probably he'll inherit the Onager estate and continue its gradual decline.

He leaves a few minutes later. Who knows where he's headed?

The freezing rain has stopped, and the sun is already out. I watch TV for a couple more hours, then walk downtown and get a sandwich. I kill time with a cup of hot chocolate at Northern Lights, one of the few hip places in the city. It's a coffee shop across from the courthouse that has things like poetry readings and folk music on the weekends. Students from the U hang out there and eat biscotti and drink espresso.

I ask the guy behind the counter if there are any job openings. He says he doesn't think so.

So I walk past the Coney Island Lunch, and I see Joey's father in there, scarfing down a hot dog.

I've got nothing to do. So I go in.

He looks up from the booth and waves at me with the stub of the hot dog. I take a seat across from him.

"So that trouble you were talking about bit you on the ass," he says.

"Yeah. It sucks."

He wipes some mustard off the corner of his mouth with his wrist. "You want one?"

"Nah," I say. "I ate."

"I'm gonna get another."

He steps up to the counter to order, then walks back over and sits down. "Your mom and dad pissed off?"

I shrug. I hold my thumb and next finger a quarter inch apart. "The house could burn down or they could win the lottery, and their expressions would change this much. So who knows what they think about this. They hardly said anything."

"Tell you what," he says. "If Joey got booted out of school, he'd hear about it big-time." Then he laughs. "His mom would tear him a new one."

"Would she?"

He rolls his eyes and shakes his head slowly. "I don't know. She finally stopped beating him up a few years ago. . . . She whacked me pretty good a few times, too."

"You never hit him?"

"Never."

"That's about what he said."

"It's true."

A waitress brings over his hot dog and asks me if I want

anything. I'm taking up space, so I figure I ought to get something. So I order a soda.

"Let me ask you something," he says. "Your dad ever have a real job?"

"What do you mean? He's a professor."

"Yeah. I mean, did he ever do anything else? Just wondering. Seems like if you're gonna teach, you'd be better at it if you did something else first, you know? Got real-world experiences. Played sports, at least."

I shake my head. "No. He didn't."

"Just was wondering. No big deal. Real-world experience means a lot."

I'm not allowed on the high school campus at all, but I walk over that way around four o'clock. From a block above, I can look down into the stadium and watch my former teammates working out, running 200-meter intervals, throwing the shot and discus on the infield, working on starts and hurdles. I can hear the coaches' whistles and the high-jump bar clanging to the ground after a miss, and I can feel the pain and the effort as guys struggle toward the finish line or try to propel themselves through the air.

I'd be the best athlete in the stadium if I was out there.

Maybe I'll run that marathon this fall after all; something to point toward, keep me focused until this is all behind me and I can start competing again for real. When I finally get to college.

But I already feel disconnected. I've spent years aiming toward this spring, my final high school track season. It's like all that preparation has been erased.

"I thought I might find you here."

I turn and see Shelly walking up the hill toward me with a tight smile. I fold my arms and nod slowly.

"Free at last," she says.

"Out on my ass is more like it."

She stands next to me and looks down at the track. "You should be out there," she says, barely above a whisper.

I nod. She sounds really sad for me, which makes me feel sad for her.

Watching practice from up here feels like one of those near-death experiences you read about, where a guy says his spirit was hovering above a crash scene, watching the paramedics pull his body out of the wreckage.

She looks down at the wobbly sidewalk, old slates pushed up at uneven angles.

I stare at the hurdlers, whacking the barriers with their feet as they strain toward the finish line. "Why'd you stop running?" I ask her. "Competing, I mean."

"Just didn't like it," she says. "I liked it when I was four-teen, but I just don't have that need to kick anyone's ass anymore. . . . The way you do."

"Yeah. Like I do."

She starts to speak, then stops. She waits another minute, then asks slowly, "How could you do that, Mike?"

"Do what?"

111

"Let yourself get so screwed over."

"What would you have done?"

"*Fought* it." She looks at me in disgust. "Tell them what happened."

"I did."

"You did what?"

"I told them what happened. I bought some joints. They got delivered to my locker. The cops found them. End of story."

She shakes her head. Her voice is subdued again. "That's not the whole story."

"It's the only part that matters."

She lets out a sigh and kicks at one of the bumps in the sidewalk. "Mr. Integrity, huh?"

"I gotta live with myself."

"Stupid." She spits the word out. Then she starts crying. I put my hand on her shoulder, and she leans into me. "Yeah," I say. "I'm stupid. But I'll get over it. So will you."

"I can't believe you let yourself get kicked out of school."

"School sucks anyway. I'll survive."

"That's great, Mike. Good luck living the rest of your life in *Scranton*."

She's got to be kidding me. This is a onetime screwup, not some pattern. "I'm not *that* stupid," I say.

"I hope not."

"Would that be so bad if I did?"

"Did what?"

"Stayed in Scranton."

She slowly starts shaking her head again. "You're better than that, Mike, and you know it."

And with that, she starts walking away. I let her go. Maybe I'll catch up to her someday.

I stand there for a long time, staring at the athletes in the stadium, unable to move from this spot. And I start thinking about what *my* obit might be like, hopefully a long time in the future.

> **Born and raised in Scranton, Michael attended Lackawanna Junior College for a year before transferring to Lock Haven University of Pennsylvania, where he excelled in cross-country and track and field. In later years, he was a three-time winner of the Steamtown Marathon.**

Down on the track, Jay and Rico are leading a pack of runners racing around the far turn. They're running steady but hard, probably a 400-meter trial. Both of them are faster than I am but not as strong.

> **He is survived by four successful children and many grandchildren and great-grandchildren.**

If I was out there, I'd be right on Rico's shoulder, pushing him along the backstretch and ready to make my move, feeling the strain but working right through it.

> He was the author of several beloved novels
> and movie scripts.

If I was out there, they'd be sweating it big-time, not just because of the work but because they'd know I was stalking them, ready to pounce.

> He traveled widely and had many friends.

And now, just before the final turn, I'd be bursting past them, kicking it into a higher gear and moving to the inside lane. They'd be straining to stick with me, but I'd be tougher; there'd be no quit in me anymore.

> He took some hard shots, but he never, ever
> gave up.

If I was out there, I'd roar onto the finishing straightaway, opening up the lead, driving hard, capitalizing on all that work I put in this winter.

That's what I'd be doing.

If I was out there.

STURBRIDGE:
AN INSIDER'S GUIDE

Half a block from the Turkey Hill convenience store, there's a town bench. And lately, if I'm not in school or at soccer practice, chances are I'm sitting there, thinking, for a lot of reasons.

For one thing, my best friend, Joey—the jerk—has a girlfriend now, the girl he knew I was after. And then there's soccer. Me and Joey are the backbone of the first strong soccer team our school's ever had, and we've got a chance to win the league this season. But that'll take teamwork, and that's the one thing we're missing.

Joey hogs the ball *and* gets the girls. But he's always been there for me—until now. Or maybe I'm just tired of being there for him. I suppose we ought to grow up. Maybe we'd win more soccer games.

"Wallace firmly establishes himself as one of the best sports novelists around for teenagers."   —*The Book Report*

"Wallace's ear for locker room banter . . . shines through in his vibrant characterizations."   —*Publishers Weekly*

A *Booklist* Top 10 Youth Sports Book

LOSING IS NOT AN OPTION
RICH WALLACE

RON IS A RUTHLESS COMPETITOR.

But he's a keen observer, too. He watches his summer-league basketball team—five guys trying to fit together on the court. He watches Dawn on the dance floor, and that tiny star tattoo on her shoulder. He watches Darby run, her legs all sweat and muscle. He watches his dad move in with his grandmother, and make do.

But he's more than a watcher: he's a hustler on the court, a poker player, a rule breaker, a poet, and a take-no-prisoners competitor on the track.

In nine interwoven stories, award-winning author Rich Wallace brings a small-town high school to life through the sharp, spare voice—and the heart-pounding defeats and triumphs—of an athlete.

"This collection of short stories by a master writer of edgy sports fiction follows a teen and the people he knows through growing up and competing in, among other things, basketball, running, and life."
—*School Library Journal*